Rover
And Other Magical Tales

Nancy Schoellkopf

ISBN-13: 978-0692648063
ISBN-10: 0692648062

For The Thursday Night Regulars

who, for better or worse, have convinced me I write funny.

CONTENTS

Rover

Blanca

Blanca was asleep. Her thick blond hair, wound into a long braid, stretched across her satiny pillowcase like a rope. Her bedroom, kitchen, and parlor smelled of late summer peaches, white peaches, peeled and diced and baked into a pie. The piecrust was hand-rolled and sprinkled with granulated sugar that shone in the moonlit kitchen like stars peeking through tree branches. Outside actual stars dotted the August sky. It was midnight.

A large white Samoyed with long slender legs ran up Blanca's driveway and leapt over her white picket fence. He pushed his slender snout between the gardenias and lilacs that grew in the narrow beds along the east side of the yellow and white cottage to rest his shiny forepaws on a wide wooden windowsill.

Inside, Bear, the black Persian cat, paced like a sentry from kitchen to pantry to bathroom hall. The scent of dog made his nose and ears twitch. He ran to the bedroom, jumped on the bed and raced across Blanca's pillow, pushing his massive face through the heavy curtains to peer out the cerulean window. He hissed and swiped at the glass. Blanca stirred.

Lifting herself on a wobbly elbow, Blanca peered out the window above her feline companion. Her own thin face cast an ivory oval on the watery surface. She leaned closer.

When the dog caught sight of Blanca, his canine frame shivered in joy, his hips, ribs and neck vibrated, all four white feet pranced and pawed at the dirt like a show horse anxious to canter. His thin pink tongue rapidly darted about his own shaggy chin and sharp black nose. He leapt onto his hind legs, his front paws batting at the air as if performing an elaborate magic trick.

Blanca buried her face in her tiny hands. "Noooooo!" she wailed. Bear the cat, startled by the depth of her emotion, leapt down from his perch and retreated under the bed. He huddled between a cedar drawer of winter woolens and a cardboard box of cook books, and he waited.

The dog dropped his long pointed snout between his front paws, squeezed his blue eyes into a neat squint and whimpered. Slowly lifting his head, he gazed at Blanca dolefully. She had eyes the color of turquoise, a steady and ancient stone. Yet her lips quivered; she was relenting. "I'll meet you at the back door," she mouthed.

When she cracked open the kitchen door, he sprang through, bursting forth with a series of short staccato barks. His long neck stretched toward the ceiling and his big jaws fell open, his thick teeth bared, laughing triumphantly.

Blanca closed and bolted the door behind him. "Steven, you woke me from a sound sleep," she scolded, and the dog responded with another series of sharp yaps. Blanca clapped her hands. "Enough!" she yelled and her voice faltered. She took a deep breath to avoid tearing up. "You need to be quiet, Steven!" She paused to swallow and the dog looked up at her expectant. "I'm going back to bed," she whispered.

He nodded, gave a final snappy yip, then raced past her dining room and through the hallway to her bedroom. In one graceful leap, he landed on the foot of her bed. Bear, already perched on the headboard, landed defiant on the mattress, raising his furry back, displaying claws and teeth.

Blanca snapped her fingers and the animals retreated to neutral corners. She stared at the dog. "I don't think so." She pointed to the floor and he obediently jumped down. "Sleep in the living room," she commanded. "And I don't mean on the couch."

The Samoyed paused in the doorway, ears pricked, gaze unwavering as Blanca eased herself back into bed, stroking the cat to calm him. She didn't want to look at Steven, but she couldn't help it. Their eyes met and the dog released a high-pitched whine, very soft, very sad, and Blanca wanted to scream. "All right," she blurted. "Just let me sleep."

The dog happily circled three times and settled onto the rug at the side of her bed. Blanca switched off the lamp and rolled toward the wall. Bear lay on the pillow by Blanca's face, his feet tucked beneath him, his whiskers drooping, but his amber eyes half open and alert: a silent sentinel shaped like an enormous loaf of brown bread.

At dawn the bedroom had a creamy pink glow as if the whole cottage had been transported to the inside of a large conch shell. Blanca opened her eyes and gazed down at Steven, still asleep on the blue and salmon colored Chinese rug, but now magically dressed in his daytime garb.

He was a tall man, six foot three, blond with high chiseled cheekbones and a thin nose. Even lying on the floor in his navy blue dress pants he didn't appear scruffy. No, he looked aristocratic, like a prince from a fairy tale. The cuffs of his pale blue shirt had been neatly folded back and tucked in to expose the fine bones of his wrists, his long-fingered hands. Staring at those hands—one pressed between his knees, the other cradling his unshaven jaw, Blanca felt an involuntary shudder between her throat and her chest, a pull of sadness, an awful hollow that seemed to open suddenly in her gut. He still awed her.

That he mysteriously transformed into a dog every night at midnight had initially proved to be somewhat of an obstacle when they were first together. He managed to hide it from her for several months, even though they were living on the same floor in the co-ed dorms. Looking back, she supposed she should have been wary of the ease with which he could lie: telling her he was gallantly demonstrating concern for her reputation by his insistence that they both be back in their own beds by twelve. But when she suggested they get their own apartment off campus (reputation be damned) he blurted out the truth. Of course she thought it was a joke; he had such a quirky sense of humor, making her sit through all those vintage Woody Allen movies. But he wasn't laughing now.

It terrified her the first time she watched his ears and snout lengthen and fur sprout on his cheeks and back. Yet when she looked into his pale blue canine eyes she knew it was him. Regardless of the vehicle, she would always recognize the spirit of the man she loved.

They did get that apartment, and Blanca was very happy there. Although she'd always been more of a cat person, his dog half didn't matter to her in the least. Most nights she slept right through his transformation. Of course Samoyeds shed something awful so she had to go over the couch with a hand vac nearly every other day. But some nights they'd stay up late and she'd give him a good brushing while they watched Jon Stewart on the Daily Show. They both enjoyed that.

They lived together nearly five years. Blanca thought they would be together forever. She couldn't be sure, but she thought it was around the time he was studying for the bar that things changed. He seemed to find fault with everything she did: she watched too much TV, she was too quiet at parties, the soup had too much onion and not enough garlic, and why weren't there any walnuts in the chocolate chip cookies? She shouldn't wait dinner for him; didn't she get it?—he was busy. This is how it is; this is how it would always be if he would ever be successful in law. She better get used to that.

Bear cried a long loud yowl and Blanca jumped. Steven's eyes flew open. "Oh, God," he murmured, sitting up. "I gotta go."

He scurried to his feet and Blanca sprang after him. Bear squealed and growled.

"That's it?" Blanca asked. "No explanation, no thank you?"

Steven turned abruptly as he strode toward the kitchen. "Did you see what I did with my car key when I came in last night?"

"For crying out loud, Steven!" She threw up her hands. "Just leave!"

"I'll call you later," he said insistently, his hand on the doorknob.

"Just leave," she repeated. "It's what you're good at."

He rolled his eyes and slammed the door. She turned away, telling herself she didn't care. Yet she ran to the front window to watch him stride down the driveway, his arms swinging in that stiff deliberate way he had when he was annoyed. He reached the sidewalk, still in his bare feet, crossed the alley to a white BMW convertible parked in front of the house next door. A beamer, and it looked new. Geez.

He climbed in, adjusted the mirror to steal a glance at himself, ran quick fingers through his hair. Must have found the key; the engine started right up. He pulled out, headed south.

Rosanna

The first time I see him is in the English pub on R Street near the railroad tracks. I go there sometimes with co-workers for a little TGIF celebration. I don't go every week, twice a month maybe. This pub has quite a variety of ales and beers. They've got this nice apricot beer from a microbrewery in the foothills. But I'm not much of a drinker. I can't keep up with some of those guys from the English Department. They're all frustrated poets, working on their great American novels and maybe they think it will improve the prose if they can't see the computer keyboard or something.

This one girl's working on a series of vampire novels and she turns me onto tomato beer—half beer/half tomato juice. I like it; it's got a little bite to it, and I can hang out a little later without getting wasted.

So one night last spring I catch sight of him—young guy with broad shoulders and slim hips, a blond beach boy type with a shaggy goatee. But he is very well dressed in a navy blue suit, and even after five on a Friday night he's sporting a tie with the crispest little Windsor knot you're ever going to see. It makes me laugh just to look at him. He looks like the worst kind of Metrosexual with slicked back hair and buffed fingernails. But he has these whimsical eyes, crinkly and kind. He has an ironic smile; the corners of his mouth draw downward when he laughs. He looks enchanting—and enchanted.

I don't talk to him that first night; we just exchange a few smiles and glances. I'm not looking for anything; it's obvious he's considerably younger than I am. Still every time I come to the pub he shows up in his neat little suit and every time he sits a little closer to our table. "He's a wild animal and you're taming him," Vampire Girl tells me. She's young, she's romantic and she's obviously got an overactive imagination, but she amuses me. "Next week," she tells me, "leave a trail of beer nuts from the entrance to your chair; he won't be able to resist."

He finally gets up his nerve to join us on the first Friday in May. His name is Steve and he works down at the Capitol for the Assembly Fish and Game Committee. Hence the suit. "Lose the tie," I tell him. "You're with the wolf pack now."

"Woo—oooo!" Vampire Girl howls obligingly, just like our students do at pep rallies and basketball games. I shake my head. She's a much better match for Steve-o than I am— they're closer in age—but the Vamp only has eyes for this guy in my department, an Advanced Placement Calculus teacher with rimless glasses and a wild mane of curly hair. He looks like a refugee from the 60s with his political T's and bumper stickers. Truth is, he irks me. We teach math to kids, for Christ's sake. If math is anything, it's apolitical. It's elegant and balanced. It can't be twisted for ulterior motives. It's beyond words, beyond the mundane. It's reliable and it's pure. In this smarmy culture, it's nice to know something is.

Anyway it surprises me to see that Steve-o is interested in me, but I'm not complaining. Guess he likes his girls big. He's almost as tall as I am and when he loosens his tie I see he's got curly hair on his chest. I like a guy with a little fur.

But like I said, I'm not looking for anything so I don't go back there just to see him. I'm busy, wrapping up the school year, so I give up the Friday beer until school starts up again in mid August. Steve-o doesn't waste any time asking me out to dinner that night. He takes me to this rib joint down on the north end of Fifteenth. The barbecue sauce is tangy and smoky. I liked it; usually those places make sauce that is way too sweet.

We end the evening back at my house in midtown. Escrow has just closed in June, so I haven't even been here two months yet, but I love the place. So for a minute I hesitate, having second thoughts about letting Steve come in. He's followed me in his own car and he has this funny look on his face when we meet on the sidewalk. "This is where you live?" he asks, and his upper lip seemed to flicker a little in disdain.

Hey, I know midtown can be a little uneven, but this is a nice block. There are some vintage Victorians up the street, and an amazing Craftsman mansion at the top of the ridge. Then I notice he's sneaking glances left and right, turning to check over his shoulder. You'd think a guy who works for the government would be up on the crime stats. We're no worse off here than Land Park or even North Natomas. "I feel very safe here," I say, wanting to reassure him. Still he seems pretty relieved when we get inside and he makes sure the shades are drawn.

After that, he seems to relax and we get along fine. He's not the fussy guy I feared he might be. He doesn't care that so many cardboard boxes still line the dining room and kitchen walls. He's satisfied with Coca Cola and hot Cheetos; he knows I hadn't been expecting guests.

More important, he seems impressed with my plans for the house. After all this is the first house I've invested in all by myself, and I'm proud to be able to afford it on a teacher's salary. Sure, when I got divorced I wanted my half of the community property, but I refused the alimony. It's a matter of pride.

I like too that Steve-o is no "yes man." He's never heard of Stickley but when I tell him about my ambition to own a few pieces of fine furniture, again he's impressed. Yet he makes it clear he thinks the prairie settee was a little small for a couple of big people like ourselves. "Big Babe," he calls me. I have to laugh. No matter. He does like the Harvey Ellis armoire in the bedroom but he makes me promise I won't get rid of my extra long double wide bed. This is easy to agree to because the man can do some amazing things with his tongue. And that's all I'll say about that.

That's why what happens next is so surprising. After we do the deed he gets up to take a shower. I hear him go into the bathroom and turn on the water, and the water runs and runs and runs. After 35 minutes I go to check on him and he's gone. Vanished. Now I'm no blushing flower, and I have to admit this isn't the first man I've brought home from a bar. But most guys have the decency to wait for you to fall asleep before they book it. Or they make up some story about having to leave at one AM to go film a meteor shower and post it on Youtube, or they've got to get up at 4:30 to drive two hours to get to the great bass fishing on the Mokelumne River. But to leave my shower running? That's a new one.

Later that same morning. . .

Blanca stood outside in the September sunshine, surveying the massive white rose vine that crept up the side of her stucco porch. She wore her old Birkenstocks and a faded blue Hawaiian shirt that used to belong to Steven. She pulled out her pruning sheers and began deadheading the roses, dropping wilted blossoms into a plastic bucket at her feet. She hummed to herself as she worked, Beach Boy tunes and melodies from Beethoven and Vivaldi.

Bear rubbed his furry head against her ankle. She turned to pat his head, sprinkling a few white petals for him to bat. She straightened up in time to see Steven parking his Beamer in front of the house near the corner. She moistened her lips and ran her fingers through her hair.

Steven got out of his car, and Blanca could see he had showered and shaved and was looking very fresh. He wore crisp khakis and a button down shirt and he had a blue and brown bag in his hand. He'd been to La Bou! Oh, they could go inside, and she could make chocolate chip pancakes. She even had some Rainer cherries. She could make clafouti!

He was approaching, his lips pursed, his jaw tight. She set the safety clasp of the pruning sheers. Her arms ached to hold him. She took a step toward him, extended her hand. "Chocolate croissants?" she asked expectantly, but he held up a warning palm like a stop sign.

"Look," he said, his words slow and deliberate. "I didn't buy these for you. I'll call you later, okay?"

Her face seemed to scrunch up, her lips and eyebrows pulling inward like fingers trying to grasp at an elusive object or idea. She shook her head. "What?"

"I'll call you later," he repeated as he brushed past her. He walked across the alley to the house adjacent to Blanca's tiny cottage, the small brick bungalow with its massive rose vine, the red blossoms as big as beach balls swaying on its slender branches.

"Where are you going?" Blanca bleated, truly confused and genuinely hurt by his rebuff.

He spoke louder this time, as if explaining something to an immigrant, some poor hapless foreigner, someone with an advanced degree maybe from a university in their own country, but who has the misfortune of being unable to speak the dominant English. "I'll Call. You. Later."

"I don't understand," she said.

He was nearly on the porch. "Can't you leave me alone? I said I'd call later."

Blanca gasped as the truth flooded into her consciousness. "You slept with her last night, didn't you? And then, after midnight! Why, you snuck out! And she doesn't know, does she?"

"We broke up nearly a year ago, Blanca," Steve said in a controlled monotone. "So, like I said, this doesn't concern you."

"It concerns me when you wake me up out of a sound sleep, Steven." Her voice was shaking now. "You're the one who made it my concern. I didn't come looking for you." Instead of pointing a scolding finger at him, she jabbed the pruning sheers in the air in his direction.

He shrugged. "Okay," he conceded in a blasé tone. "I'm sorry."

His nonchalant apology seemed to light a fire under her. "Do you think I want to be concerned about you?" she blurted, her eyes streaming. "Do you think I want to still be in love with you? Do you think I want that?"

"Fine, Blanca," he yelled back. "Play the victim. But you don't love me. You never did."

Her mouth dropped open. "How can you say that? You know..."

He stepped back toward her to confront her across the alley. "I know you never loved me. I know it. And you want to know how I know it? I know if you'd loved me—truly loved me—the spell would have been broken."

"You're blaming me?"

"I'm not blaming you; I'm stating facts. That's how it works. That's how it always works. Love breaks the spell. And you couldn't break the spell."

She began to sob in earnest, her hands loose at her sides, the pruning sheers dropped on the asphalt, her hair pushed back behind her ears to expose her red chapped cheeks and lips as she bawled loud and unashamed.

She turned suddenly to run into the house but he grabbed her arm. "Blanca, wait," he said. "I'm sorry." He meant it too; she could see that. That diagonal line that cut across his forehead when he got angry or scared—that was gone. And that muscle in his jaw that twitched when he was sad or sorry—that was twitching. She let him hold her arm and her gaze for a moment. She let him talk.

"You understand," he was saying, "why I had to leave? I need to find somebody who can change me back."

She pulled away gently. "It doesn't matter to me who or what you are. I love you exactly as you are. I don't care if you're a dog."

He stepped back from her "I care," he said. "I care."

Rosanna

I get up early most Saturdays to hit the gym and--okay, then the muffin shop. But not today. Today I'm taking my time. I make myself an omelette with cheddar cheese and green salsa and I'm hanging out at the kitchen table, working on my third cup of coffee and I'm thinking maybe I'll go online and start pricing granite counter tops because I don't know if I can stand this baby blue tile in here one more minute, when I hear a crash, like metal hitting concrete. It wasn't really loud, but still I'm worried that it's a car accident in the alley, so I stand up to peek out. There's Steve-o out near the sidewalk and he's talking to my neighbor—I can't remember her name—Brenda, Bianca—something Italian or Spanish, I think. She's an awfully sweet little girl—well, that sounded condescending, didn't it? I didn't mean it that way. She's in her mid 20s, I think, and she's got a good job. She told me she's the pastry chef at Maryann's Kitchen on 35th and J. I love that place, especially in the winter. They've got the best soups and stews. I'm not much for sweets, but I did have an apricot cobbler there once that was wonderful. I told this girl—Blanca, that's it, Blanca. I told Blanca how much I enjoyed that and she made me a big old pan of it and brought it over one night last July. Isn't that sweet? I had a piece of it then put it in the freezer. Now that school's started I should thaw it out and take in into the staff room. I'll be the hit of the next math department meeting.

But now here's Steve-o out there on the sidewalk with her. I didn't think I'd see him again but here he is with Blanca. I can't hear them but it looks like she's crying. Her pruning sheers are on the ground.

Blanca is such a tiny thing, barely five foot two or three. She looks like a little boy with her round shoulders and her little breasts and butt. A little boy with a mass of dramatic blond hair. I suppose men are drawn to that, as well as her sweetness; for she seems genuinely sweet, kind and unspoiled. Probably naïve, yes, but unpretentious, without guile.

Hey, here's something: Steve is moving closer and taking her arm. What is going on? I decide to get a better look so I move to the front of the house.

Blanca's eyes are red and Steve's jaw is quivering. Well, you don't have to be Doctor Phil to figure this one out. They each take a step back; Blanca seems headed for her porch. I can't let this chance slip by: I grab the knob and fling open my front door.

"Steve!" I blurt cheerfully. "What a surprise! And Blanca! So good to see you sweetie!" I step down onto the sidewalk and give her a little hug; I want to reassure her. "How are you?" I ask.

Blanca blushes a bit. "I'm okay, Rosanna," she says. "It got warm all of a sudden so I'm going inside."

I clasp her hand before she can escape. "Your rose vine looks amazing, Blanca. I need to clip mine back too."

"Oh, I could do that for you," she offers.

"I have an idea," I say. "Why don't we do it together? One evening next week. Then I can take you out to dinner."

"You don't have to—"

"I insist. Say Monday? At six? It'll be fun." I glance over at Steve. He looks like he might vomit.

"Okay," Blanca is saying. "I look forward to it."

"Great," I say releasing her hand. "Sooo--you know my friend Steve-o."

"We met in college," Steve interjects quickly.

"Steve-o?" Blanca repeats the moniker as if she finds it distasteful.

Steve manages a weak smile. "Blanca knew me as Steven." He pauses. "That's what the professors called me."

I swear, if looks could kill, Steve would be lying dead in the alley right now, because I shoot him a glare as cold and steely as an ice pick to the wind pipe. The gall—like I don't have eyes. As if the two of them have never met outside a college classroom.

The corners of Blanca's mouth are melting into her chin like jelly. This poor girl is so fragile--like a figurine made of very thin glass—no, like a Beleek tea cup. My grandmother had a set of four of these Irish tea cups, but only one had no cracks. Unspoiled porcelain. Very rare, very precious.

I squeeze her shoulder. "You know, Blanca, you are too thin. I don't know how you can make such luscious pastries and stay so svelte! I am going to help you bulk up this fall and winter."

Blanca laughs, obviously uncomfortable. "Oh, I don't need that!"

Then I get serious on her. "You do need that," I say. "You need some muscle." I look into her pale eyes and she gazes back at me. She may not understand completely, but she nods. She's beginning to trust me.

"Well," I say, "Steve and I have some catching up to do. I'll see you Monday, Blanca."

I turn to Steve and my voice takes on the tone I use when a kid hasn't turned in his homework. "Let's go, Steve." I point to the door and he obediently trots inside.

I slam the door. "Sit," I command, pointing to the old chenille chair. He complies. I waste no time. "You are such a dog," I accuse.

His eyes bulge. "How did you know?" He sounds panicked. "Blanca told you, didn't she?"

"Oh, come on, Steve-o. It should be obvious I have been around the block more than a few times, and I don't need anybody to tell me that you are the worst kind of hound dog there is."

He lowers his eyes and stares at his hands. He looks humbled. But then he says something that surprises me. He barely glances up and he says, "Actually I'm a Samoyed."

"What?"

"Samoyeds aren't hounds. We're a working breed. You know, herding."

I feel my lips scrunching into a knot. Is he nuts? "Whatever," I say. "A dog is a dog and I know you're a dog. All that crap about meeting in college."

"We did meet in college."

"I don't doubt that. And the profs called you 'Steven.' Good for you. But after that you and Blanca had a relationship. A serious relationship. And you are a dog not to see how much she still loves you."

He stands up. "No, that's not true. I mean, well, it is true that we had a relationship, but—"

"But nothing, you dog! She still loves you."

"No, no, she doesn't." He coughs, lifting his hand to his mouth and I see that white fur is rapidly sprouting on his wrist and forearm, spreading onto his hand. I gasp. I take a step back.

"Oh, my God," I exclaim. "You are an actual dog! I was speaking metaphorically!" I had to laugh then. "You are a real dog." His nose is getting long and so is his fur. I'll bet that's rough in summer. "Oh, my, you *are* a Samoyed!"

He's coughing quite vigorously, beginning to stoop over. "You think this is funny?"

"Oh relax," I say, sinking into my prairie settee. "My ex husband was a skunk. Try living with that." I shake my head, remembering. "You know I went to college in Texas and I dated a football player who turned into an armadillo every night. Now that was interesting." I gaze out the window, feeling wistful. "He was a line backer."

Steve's transformation is nearly complete, but he can still talk, even as his tongue grows longer. "You've seen this before?"

I shrug. "Many times. It's nothing to worry about."

"But it's daytime. This only happens at night."

"Progress, Steve-o," I assure him. "Things evolve. You'll see."

He's quite hoarse but he continues. "You can see why I had to leave Blanca."

"No," I say. "I don't get that at all. Why did you leave Blanca?"

But all he can do is bark now, so my question is left unanswered. We sit for a long time, just staring at each other. I can't help it: I'm feeling quite smug.

"It's going to be fine, Steve-o. No worries." I saunter into the kitchen and get the leash. I've had a collection of pets over the years. I'd never get rid of this leash.

He tries to resist me at first. "Trust me, Steve," I say. "You really have no choice." He finally let me fasten it on, and then we go out for a walk. It really is a lovely day.

Monday Evening

Rosanna stood in the evening sunlight, pruning sheers in hand as she confronted the hearty tendrils that stretched up and across her brick porch. She didn't like to admit it, but this massive vine was one of the main reasons she had been attracted to the house in the first place. This one and the rose vine that grew up Blanca's stucco porch on the other side of the alley. The houses were very different in style, the rose blossoms varied in color, fragrance and size, but the shape of the vines and the direction of their growth created a perfect symmetry that Rosanna found intriguing and irresistible. She wondered if the two houses had shared the services of a single gardener, an artistic soul who had trained the two plants in their twin growth. Or had it been the mysterious randomness of nature that led sun-seeking blossoms to adopt similar patterns? Whether random or designed, Rosanna found the vines magnificent. She stepped closer, grabbed a wilted blossom in her fingers and clipped.

Blanca rode up on her bike a few minutes later. "Sorry," she said. "Work ran late."

"No problem," Rosanna assured her. "Take your time."

Blanca didn't see Steve stretched in a docile recline on Rosanna's porch, but Steve saw her. He batted his eyes and thumped his tail.

"I'll go get my clippers," she began, then she saw the dog. He stood up, shivering in joy, but Blanca's hand flew to her mouth in horror. "Steven!" she exclaimed. Then her eyes grew wide, realizing she may have revealed a secret. She turned rapidly to gauge Rosanna's reaction, but the older woman only patted her shoulder.

"That's okay, honey," Rosanna said. "That's Steve."

Blanca couldn't move, she was so shocked. "But it's daylight," she managed to whisper.

"Don't worry about it," Rosanna said, as she returned to clipping. "My guess is the spell will soon resolve itself. That's why Steve is spending more time as his dog self. He's working on it."

"Spending more time?" Blanca repeated. "You make it sound like he's choosing this!"

Rosanna turned to look at Blanca. "I'm sure it doesn't feel like a choice," Rosanna agreed. "But Steve wants the spell broken, and look—the universe is obliging him! It's led him straight to your door."

Blanca widened her stance on the sidewalk and her hands drifted down from her face to clasp each other near her heart. Steve still stared at her and he began to whimper. Rosanna clipped away. "Can I pet him?" Blanca asked meekly.

Rosanna laughed. "Well of course you can! You don't have to ask my permission. He's not *my* dog."

Blanca hesitated. "He's not *my* dog either."

"No," Rosanna agreed. "He needs to learn to be his own dog. And his own man." She paused. "But if he could belong to anybody, he'd want to belong to you."

Blanca shook her head quickly. "Oh, no, that's not true." She stopped, afraid she would cry. She swallowed hard. "He needed to leave. He explained that to me."

Rosanna abruptly stopped her pruning. "Really? What did he say?"

Blanca chewed on the corner of her lip. Her voice was barely audible. "He said if I truly loved him, the spell would be broken. So he needed to find someone who loved him enough."

"He told you that? Oh, Steve-o!" She leaned down toward the dog. "You are way stupider than I thought!" Steve lay down, positioning his front paws protectively over his snout. Rosanna turned again to her neighbor. "Blanca, sweetie, that simply isn't true. Listen, from what I've seen, a spell like this comes on like a virus, but you have to be predisposed. It happens to people who are hunting in the dark, wanting to learn something about their true nature. It has nothing to do with anyone else."

Blanca stared at Rosanna. "I don't understand," she said. "What could he learn by turning into a dog?"

"Well," Rosanna said as she continued to clip, "he's the only one who can discover what that is." She leaned back to face Blanca. "I can't be sure, but if I had to guess, I'd say he needs to learn loyalty."

"Loyalty?"

"There's nothing more loyal than a dog! Of course if he'd been smart, he would have learned it from you. You seem to have loyalty to spare."

A tear slid down Blanca's cheek. "How do you know all this?" she asked.

Rosanna spread her hands wide. "I know it because I'm awake. Because I've spent a long time teaching myself to keep my eyes open, to see things as they actually are." She gestured toward the vine. "I think I got all the dead heads. Do you see any?"

"Oh, I didn't help at all," Blanca lamented.

Rosanna waved her hand and laughed. "We're not done yet. Let's clip some fresh flowers from both our vines. I'll bet the red and white roses will look amazing together."

Blanca nodded. "Okay."

"We'll pick enough for two bouquets. One for each of our houses."

"That'll be great."

Just then Bear the cat meandered down Blanca's driveway. He yowled and flicked his ears and rubbed on Blanca's ankles. Blanca picked him up, nuzzling her nose against his furry back. "Hey, Baby," she whispered.

Rosanna reached over to scratch a feline ear. "Such a beautiful cat." Bear gave a short "mao" as if acknowledging her compliment. Rosanna pointed a finger in his direction. "Yes, you are an amazing animal. I'd like to get to know you better."

Bear leaned toward the older woman and Blanca felt a sudden stab of adrenaline in her throat as she looked at the large, grumpy cat she thought she knew. Feeling a little dizzy she set the cat down gently near Rosanna's feet. "I'll get my clippers," she said.

As she headed down the driveway her curiosity got the better of her and she turned to see Bear leaping into Rosanna's arms. "Yes, you may be the one for me," she heard Rosanna whisper.

Blanca stumbled on a rock, but managed to catch herself. The eastern sky was brown and orange; fire in the foothills nearby. Acrid smoke stung Blanca's eyes but she resolved to keep them open.

Birdie's Hat

Birdie liked the new place.

The last place smelled like dirt, and the horizon was the color of mushrooms. Trees were black with large overarching branches and leaves bigger than Birdie's head. All it would take, Birdie used to think, is for one soggy leaf to fall on top of my face, and I'd probably drown.

The new place had lots of light and water. Houses were yellow and white and blue. The sky was so sharp that Birdie had to squint when she came outside, she had to put her hand up flat above her eyebrows like a native scout, and she'd tread lightly over the lawn as if she were on a quest. Towering over pine trees were mountains that were so crisp and brown they reminded Birdie of gingerbread cookies with snowy white frosting. Triangle-shaped gingerbread cookies.

Birdie liked to think about triangles and squares, geometry and mountains and the color of cookies. Papa told her it was good to notice how things were shaped, the color and form, he said. Papa was an artist. He worked on large canvases, and he said Birdie would be a great artist one day too.

Papa always gave Birdie very specific, practical advice about her artwork, like how to use the light to emphasize a shape or highlight an object. Mama gave advice too, but it was often big booming statements that Birdie didn't understand. She said Birdie had incredible "potential," that yes, of course, her talent could protect her, but someday it would also be a "great force for change in the world." Until that day, Mama said, it was best to be quiet, not to brag or show off too much.

Advice like this made Birdie miss Papa even more than she already did. Mama said Papa would come back someday. She said she was working on getting him back. She told Birdie not to worry. It had nothing to do with Birdie. It was just Mama and Papa arguing about art. Mama was an artist too, but she said she was moving beyond painting now, beyond "flat surfaces." She was creating sculpture now.

Birdie was used to new places because she and Mama moved a lot. The places were always different but the schools were pretty much the same: long squat buildings, cube shaped rooms, narrow windows near the ceiling so you couldn't see outside, and tarry black-topped playgrounds with few bushes or trees. Birdie found this institutional sameness comforting because the people were always different, as if they had just been made fresh from dough that morning, coming out of the oven to discover Birdie in their midst, a stranger with a strange name and a floppy white knit hat pulled down to her eyebrows. Mama told the teachers that Birdie had to wear her hat at all times. Funny thing was that most times nobody even asked why. "They think you have a medical issue," Mama told her, "or they think that you have to cover your head for religious reasons. Doesn't matter what they think. If anyone asks, tell them it's private."

Birdie didn't want to tell them anything. She was tempted to chirp like a parakeet to discourage anyone from approaching her at all. But Mama told her to be friendly, and Birdie always tried.

Birdie liked to spend her first recess hunting for a piece of gray concrete where she could draw with her chalk. It was her favorite thing to do. When she found a flat surface near the classroom or office where she could put her mark, then she felt at home.

Roy Armstrong was easily bored, one of those kids who found school work so easy that he seldom bothered, so his teachers thought he must be finding it all too hard. Consequently Roy was a little bit angry most of the time. Birdie noticed that Roy was tall for his age with a head like a block. He had a shock of blue-black hair and a nose like a radish. She noticed he liked to push people in line. She was none too happy to see him sauntering in her direction at lunch recess.

After a week of going unnoticed on her patch of concrete, drawing tiny chalk magpies and caterpillars, Birdie was letting loose with a large portrait of a pink and gray African elephant. Its ears were as buoyant as kites and his massive legs were sturdy as tree trunks. She was particularly proud of the rib cage; so few people appreciated the curving sweep of a mammal's rib cage, she thought, as she added a bit of black shading. The she saw Roy, sneering at her as she crouched on the ground. He didn't seem to notice her drawing. He was glaring at her head.

"What's with that hat?" he shot at her.

Birdie felt her face flush and her scalp itch. Her hand involuntarily reached for the white knit cap she always wore. Her lips tightened and she could say nothing.

"What's your problem?" Roy persisted. "You some kind of dyke or something? I'll bet only dykes wear hats that ugly."

Birdie didn't know what a dyke was, but she knew Roy wasn't paying her a compliment. She faced him defiantly. "I wear this hat to cover my hair," she said. "Mama says I have to."

"Oh, ho!" he shouted. "Your hair's so ugly your mom don't want nobody to see it."

"That's not true," she yelled back, but then she remembered what Mama had said. "It's private," she added in a small voice. "My hair is private. Now you go leave me alone!"

"Sure," he hissed, but then he rushed at her and grabbed the white hat off her head. He heard her gasp at his sudden assault, then he saw her magnificent mane of thick blond hair, sweeping down across her shoulders, nearly reaching to her waist. So pale, it was nearly white. It reflected sunlight like the surface of a pool, and tiny blue and green sparks seemed to shoot forth from each strand.

For a moment he stood, slack jawed and amazed, then she was at him, her small hand on his chest, frantically trying to grab her hat back away from him. He lifted the hat high above his own head, so she could not reach. He grinned as he watched the sparks dropping down onto her pink and gray drawing.

Suddenly a real live elephant popped up off the sidewalk and charged at him. His mouth dropped open, his eyes bulged and the hat slipped from his fingers. In a single instant, the elephant wrapped him in its trunk and stuffed him into its mouth.

"Oh, no," Birdie cried as she stooped down to pick up her hat. "I'm going to get into such trouble." The elephant sneezed and Roy Armstrong shot out of its nose.

"I told you I need to cover my hair," Birdie scolded as she pulled on the cap and stuffed her locks inside. But Roy didn't hear her. He was halfway across the play yard before she finished her sentence.

When the hat was back in place, the elephant floated back to the pavement. Birdie glanced around. Maybe no one had noticed.

The next day, Birdie drew an elaborate yellow and black tiger on the concrete in front of the office. The tiger had shoulders and hips as graceful as the wings of a bird; its paws were large but lithe like the pointed toes of a ballet dancer. Even his long skinny tail was as beautiful and velvety as a hair ribbon. Birdie was very proud of this drawing. She stood to admire it, brushing the chalk dust from her fingers and palms.

Jack Armstrong, Roy's older and taller brother, strode up. Birdie knew he was Roy's brother. He had blue-black hair and a radishy nose, just like Roy. Roy followed at a distance, puffing out his chest and sticking out his chin as if to feign a bravery he did not feel.

Jack lifted his shoulders to his ears, as if wanting to look bigger. He sneered at Birdie. "Roy says you got some kind of magic hat."

Birdie took a step back, determined not to get angry. "No," she said. "That's not true."

"You calling my brother a liar?" Jack said, thrusting his big jaw toward her like a Rottweiler. "We'll see about that!" He reached forward and grabbed the hat from her head. He turned slowly to toss the knit cap nonchalantly to his brother. "Here, Roy," he said casually but the tiger was already upon him. He saw the expansive whites of his little brother's terrified eyes. Then the hat dropped to the ground as the tiger swallowed Jack whole.

"I told you," Birdie said to Roy as she snatched up the hat, "it's not the hat that's magic, it's my hair. Mama says I have to keep it covered."

Roy stood frozen, eyes riveted on the tiger smacking its lips with its long pink tongue as Birdie shoved her hair back inside the hat. The tiger melted onto the sidewalk again. Jack Armstrong sat dazed on top of the chalk drawing. "What happened?" he murmured as the recess bell rang. Birdie skipped away.

The next afternoon Birdie strolled across the school parking lot and into Chalk Mountain Park, taking the shortcut home. She passed basketball courts and a rose garden. She was heading into a stand of conifers when someone jumped out from behind a hedgerow and tackled her. She lay face down in the dirt, struggling to get up but someone was holding her down.

"Get her hands, Tim!" It was the voice of Jack Armstrong coming from his perch on her back. A pair of gigantic feet clad in black and white running shoes--which presumably belonged to the boy named Tim—appeared before her chin. The boy now kneeled before her and she saw a large moon face grinning and leering at her as his hands reached over to hold down her arms.

"You're on, Roy," Jack said and Birdie could feel another body pressing against her shoulder blades. She heard a sound, clicking like castanets, and it filled her with dread. "What are you doing?" she screamed, though she already knew. "Stop it!"

"Hold still," Roy Armstrong berated her. "You don't want me to cut you, do ya?" All three boys laughed.

Birdie knew what was happening and she couldn't help it: she started to cry. "I'm going to get in such trouble," she whimpered. Again her pleas were met with callous guffaws.

"There!" Roy proclaimed finally. "I've got it!" Three pairs of hands simultaneously released her and three bodies pulled themselves to their feet. Birdie looked up quickly to see Roy fastening a rubber band around her now detached mane to tie it into a long ponytail. "Now I've got it," he announced. "I've got the magic hair!" The other boys leaned close to examine the yellow locks.

Birdie sat up slowly, lifting her hands to feel her hair, now bobbed unevenly around her earlobes. She sighed deeply, shaking her head. "I tried to tell you--" she began.

"Shut up," Roy countered with a laugh. But suddenly he was shrieking as the rope in his hand transformed into a creature with a slithering tongue and a hooded nape. He tried to drop it, but it adhered to his fingers as the sinister head thrust forward and bit first Jack in the neck and then Tim on the cheek. Both boys keeled back, panting and clutching their wounds. Unable to let go, Roy was helpless as the boa shot two—four—six times around his chest and slowly began to squeeze.

Birdie stood, observing the tragic scene, running her fingers through her short chopped locks. She massaged her scalp vigorously. "What a relief to be rid of that hair!" she exclaimed with a deep exhalation. "Of course it will have grown back by tomorrow, but gee!—it feels good now." She nodded to the snake, now coiled at her feet. "I tried to tell them, didn't I? I tried to warn them, but they wouldn't listen." The snake bowed its head, a farewell gesture perhaps, then it shimmied away from three still bodies and up a pine tree. "It wasn't my fault," Birdie pleaded to the retreating snake. She picked up her hat and stuffed it in her jacket pocket. "I wonder if we'll have to move again?" she mused aloud as she skipped toward home.

Mr. Moon Meets the Neighbors

Mr. Moon worked the night shift. Most days he'd be traipsing into his apartment building around dawn, feeling dull and heavy as a pile of rocks, and he'd drag himself onto the elevator before anybody else in the place was even awake. He never met any of his neighbors because he was sleeping when they were awake and he was awake when they were sleeping. He didn't care. His work was demanding and he needed to focus on that.

One evening he was headed out to work kind of early, but still late enough that most everybody else was inside their apartments parked in front of their TV's or their refrigerators for the night. He was in the elevator headed down when it stalled.

He didn't know what to do. If he didn't get to work, who would provide the gravitational pull on the oceans to make the tides come in? And if the tides didn't come in, what would happen to the jet stream that brought the warm front that caused the rain in the valley? He knew it was arrogant to think of himself as indispensable, but well, there it was. It was particularly awkward because he happened to be full this night. Light was beaming all over the tiny elevator, and seeping out into the elevator shaft.

"Hey!" he heard a voice yell. "You okay in there?"

Mr. Moon cleared his throat, but as was his habit, he maintained a stoic silence.

More voices followed.

"Who is this loony?" he heard someone say.

"What's he got?—a search light in there?"

"Hey, Marge—you gotta come see this!"

Mr. Moon heard laughter, squeals and the rolling thunder of stomping feet, both from the floors above him and floors below. It seemed his moonbeams were drawing the tenants out from all over the building.

The sharp report of metal on metal pierced Mr. Moon's ears. He leaned against the back wall as the banging continued. A sudden lurch and the elevator sprang into action again.

The rumble of loud voices hushed into a low hum of whispers as the car neared the ground floor. Mr. Moon felt a pang of anxiety, wondering what crowd had gathered in the lobby.

The elevator arrived. The doors parted. He stood before his neighbors in all his round brilliant glory. They gasped at the sight of him, so white and luminous. Their pale faces grew long and pointed and shaggy. They stooped down on all fours and howled and bayed and yipped in delight.

Mr. Moon smiled. "My kind of people," he thought, and together they drifted out, into the night.

Nancy Schoellkopf

ABOUT THE AUTHOR

Nancy Schoellkopf is the author of the critically acclaimed *Yellow-Billed Magpie,* a novel of spiritual promise. She has been telling stories and writing poems for many lifetimes. It goes without saying she's needed a second income, so this time around she's happily taught amazing children in special education classes in two urban school districts in Sacramento, California. A full time writer now, she enjoys lavishing attention on her cat, her garden and her intriguing circle of family and friends.

Contact her through her website: www.nancyschoellkopf.com.